Text copyright © 2017 by Derrick Barnes
Illustrations copyright © 2017 by Gordon C. James

All rights reserved. No part of this book may be reproduced or transmitted in any form or by any means, electronic or mechanical, including photocopying, recording, or by any information storage and retrieval system, without express written permission from the publisher.

Printed in China

Crown
ISBN 13: 978-1-57284-224- 3
ISBN 10: 1-57284-224-5
eISBN 13: 978-1- 57284-808-5
eISBN 10: 1-57284-808-1

First printing: October 2017

10 9 8 7 6 5 4 3 2 1   17 18 19 20 21

Bolden Books is an imprint of Agate Publishing. Agate books are available in bulk at discount prices. Learn more at agatepublishing.com.

To Silas Nathaniel, aka Nestle Snipes.
#BarnesBrothersForever
—DERRICK BARNES

To my son, Gabriel, and his barber, Mr. Reggie.
—GORDON C. JAMES

When it's your turn in the chair, you stand at attention and forget about who you were when you walked through that door.

You came in as a lump of clay,
a blank canvas, a slab of marble.
But when my man is done with you,
they'll want to post you up in a museum!

That's my word.

Who knows? You might just smash that geography exam tomorrow and rearrange the entire principal's honor roll.
A fresh cut does something to your brain, right?
It hooks up your intellectual.

You're a star.
    A brilliant, blazing star.
Not the kind that you'll find on a sidewalk in Hollywood.
Nope. They're going to have to wear shades
when they look up to catch your shine.

He'll lean you back in the chair,
dab that cool shaving cream on your forehead,
and then craft a flawless line with that razor—
slow, steady, surgical.
   It frames your swagger.

The cute girl in the class across the way
won't be able to keep her pretty eyes off of you.
Her friends will giggle and whisper, "Girllll . . . he's so fine!"
Yeah. That's what they'll say.

The whole school will be seasick from the rows and rows of ripples.
You'll have more waves on your head than the Atlantic Ocean.
 (Shout out to my do-rag and patience.)

There's a dude to the left of you
with a faux-hawk, deep part, skin fade.
He looks presidential.
Maybe he's the CEO of a tech company that manufactures cool.
He's a boss.
That's how important he looks.

There's a dude standing in the mirror that can't get over
the masterful designs crafted on the side of his dome.
Everywhere he goes, people will ask for his autograph.
    He looks that FRESH!
He looks like he owns a few acres of land on Saturn.
Maybe there's a river named after him on Mars.
    He looks that important.

There are two dudes, one with locs, the other with cornrows, and a lady with a butterscotch complexion, and all they want is a "shape up," "tapered sides," "a trim," and a crisp but subtle line.
And sometimes in life, that's all you ever need.
    A crisp but subtle line.

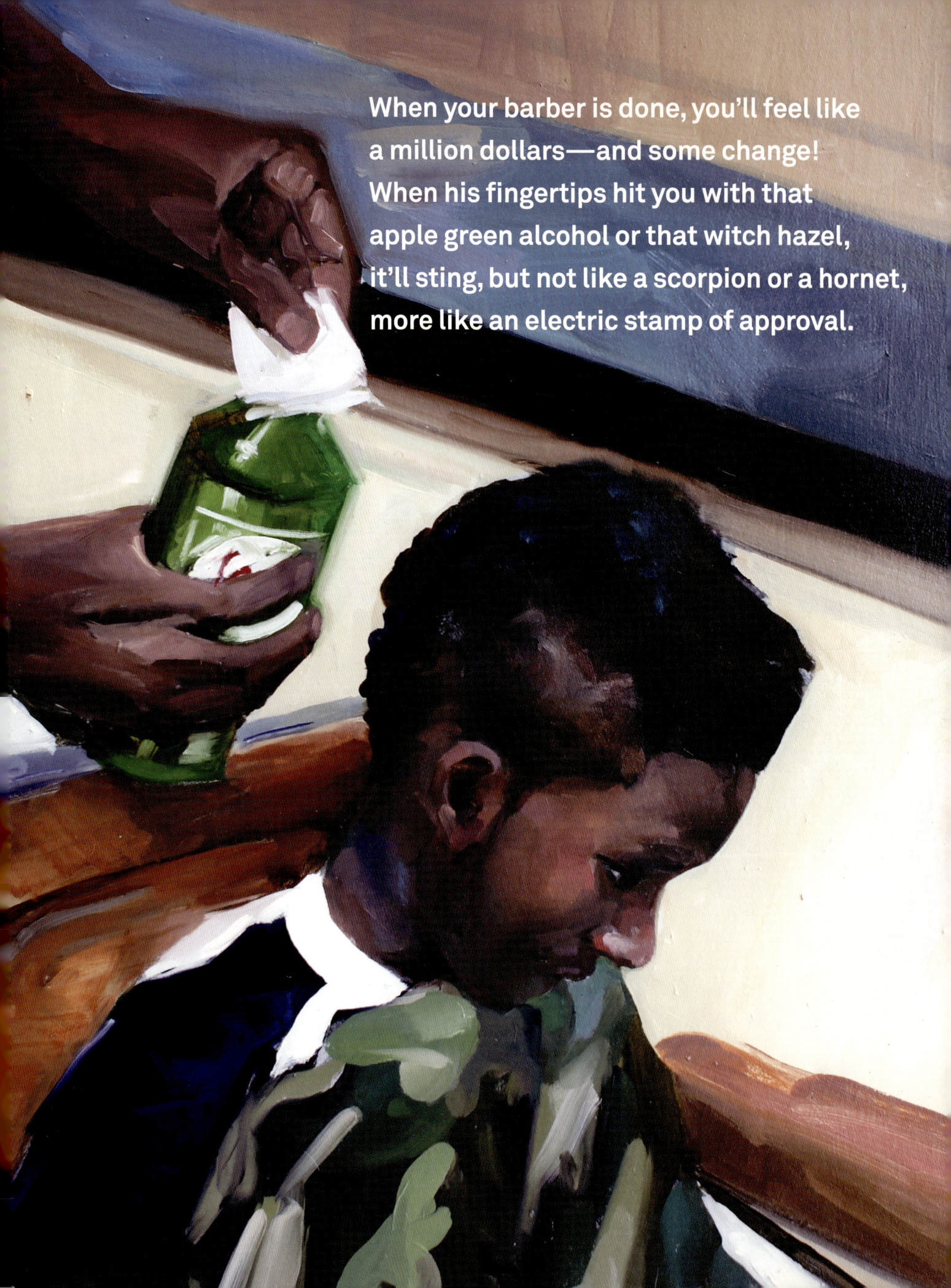

When your barber is done, you'll feel like a million dollars—and some change! When his fingertips hit you with that apple green alcohol or that witch hazel, it'll sting, but not like a scorpion or a hornet, more like an electric stamp of approval.

And when you see the cut yourself,
in that handheld mirror,
you'll smile a really big smile.
That's the you that you love the most.
That's the you that wins—everything.
That's the gold medal you.

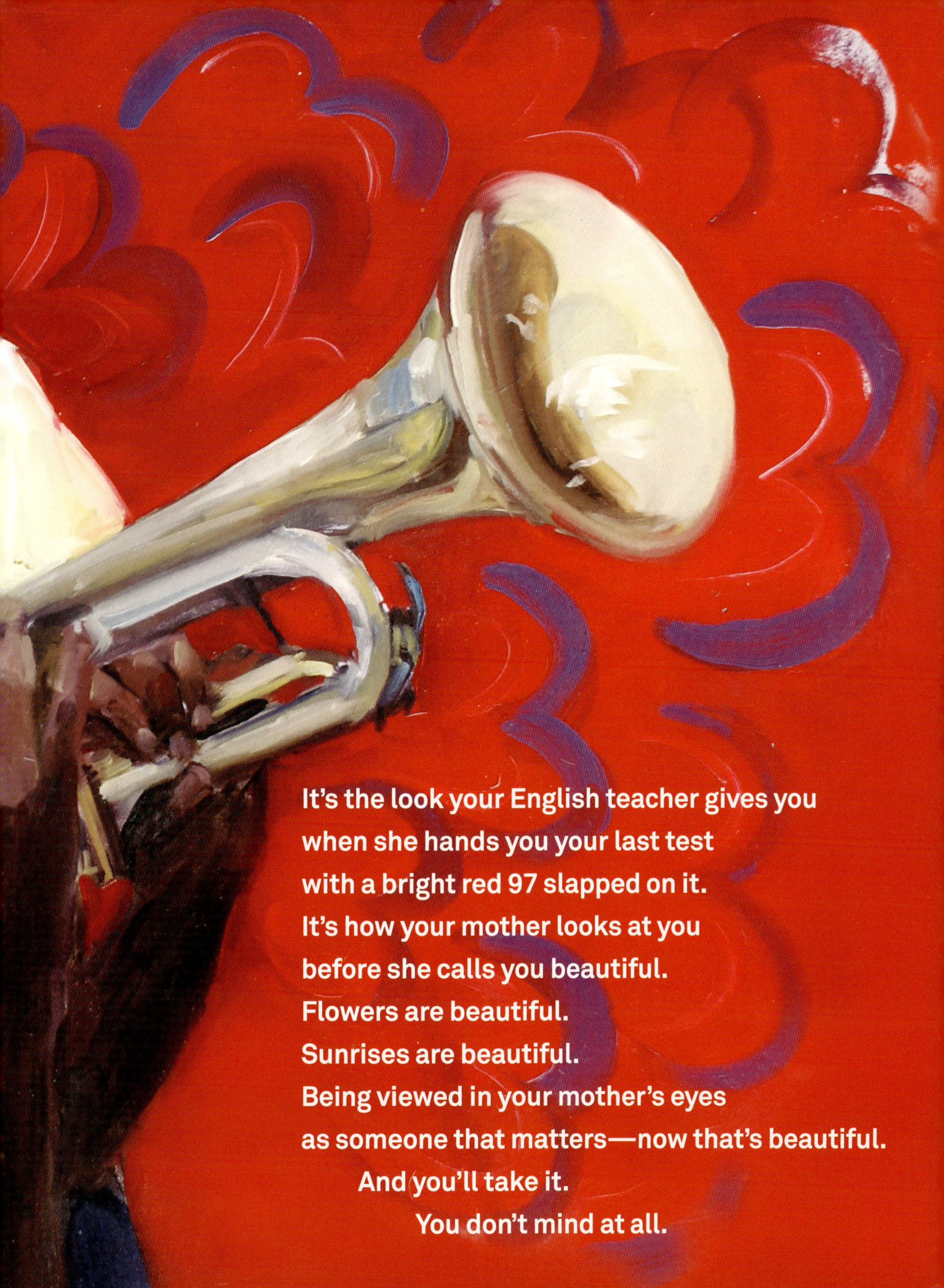

It's the look your English teacher gives you when she hands you your last test with a bright red 97 slapped on it. It's how your mother looks at you before she calls you beautiful. Flowers are beautiful. Sunrises are beautiful. Being viewed in your mother's eyes as someone that matters—now that's beautiful. And you'll take it. You don't mind at all.

Finally, he'll remove your cape, then swipe you down with a brush made from a golden horse tail.